P9-BZY-722

DATE DUE

052298

2/91

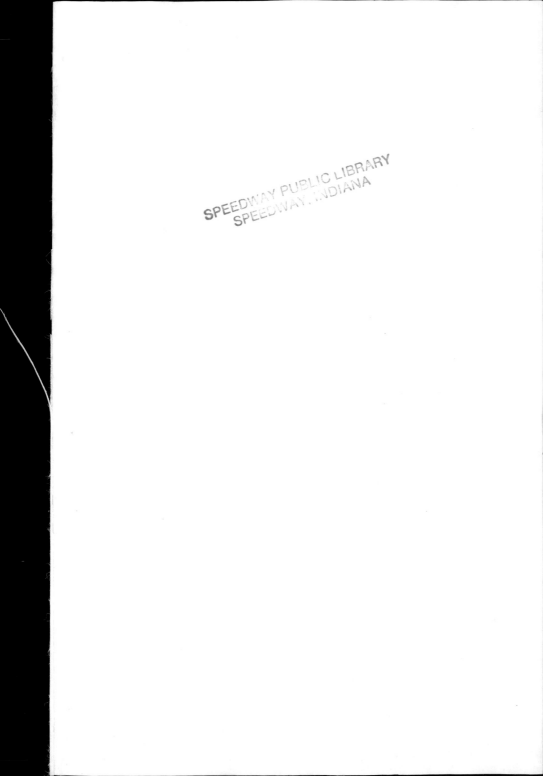

Harvey's
Wacky Parrot
Adventure

Harvey's Wacky Parrot Adventure

Eth Clifford

Houghton Mifflin Company
Boston   1990

Library of Congress Cataloging-in-Publication Data

Clifford, Eth, 1915–
  Harvey's wacky parrot adventure / by Eth Clifford.
      p.   cm.
  Summary: Harvey and his least favorite cousin Nora become
embroiled in the search for a hidden treasure somewhere in Uncle
Buck's house, with the only clue to its location held by a
loudmouthed parrot.
  ISBN 0–395–53352–X
  [1. Buried treasure—Fiction.   2. Cousins—Fiction.   3. Parrots—
  Fiction.]   I.   Title.
PZ7.H62214Hau   1990   89–39594
[Fic]—dc20   CIP
                             AC

Printed in the United States of America
BP   10 9 8 7 6 5 4 3 2 1

For our own small SCBW group

Lee, Vivian, Opal, Marilyn,
Juanita and Joy

with love

Contents

Harvey's
Wacky Parrot
Adventure

1

In which the reader meets Sinbad

"Freeze! Nobody move! I've got you covered!" The voice was low and raspy and bone-chilling. *"Take one step and you're dead!"*

My cousin Nora screamed and shot out of her chair. Then she realized who had spoken. It was Sinbad, my uncle Buck's gray African parrot. Nora sent me a sheepish glance and sat down again.

I covered my mouth with my hand to hide an ear-to-ear smile.

"Who'd you think it was?" I asked. I couldn't help laughing. I guess that was mean of me. A talking parrot was new to her.

"I knew it was Sinbad all the time, Harvey Willson." Nora's mouth tightened. "I just forgot, that's all."

I should explain about Sinbad. He's wild about TV. He sits on my uncle Buck's shoulder and the two of them watch detective thrillers for hours. At least that's what they do when they stay with us during the Christmas holidays. I suppose they do the same thing when they're in Uncle Buck's house.

I like Uncle Buck. He has the kind of smiling round face that makes him *look* permanently cheerful. A wisp of gray beard in the center of his chin is like a thin exclamation mark. His eyebrows are dashes of gray over his eyes, with droopy ends that give him an Oriental cast. A circle of gray hair rounds the base of his head and wanders up over and above his ears. His lips turn up at the corners even when he's unhappy. Mom says he could pose for a statue of a merry Buddha.

Uncle Buck has been coming to our house for years at Christmas time. I think he'd rather stay home. He's never been married, but he does have a housekeeper — Myrtle Crump. So he isn't really alone. But Mom says holidays are for families to be together, whether they like it or not.

Of course, Mom's been polite and invited Myrtle Crump as well, but both of them are happy when Myrtle Crump refuses.

"I'm not big on family gatherings," Myrtle Crump always says. And Mom is always relieved.

"There's so *much* of her," Mom explains. "She just seems to fill every room she's in."

My cousin Nora was with us because her mom and dad were away on a cruise. How my uncle Clarence ever got my aunt Mildred on a boat is a deep mystery, because Aunt Mildred is the champion worrier and nailbiter in the universe.

When my dad brought Nora home from the airport two days before Christmas, she staggered upstairs to my room without a word to anyone. I guess I should explain that Mom usually turns my room over to guests because it's closest to the bathroom. And if a guest should object and murmur something about putting me out of my room, Mom purrs, "Not at all. Harvey doesn't mind the least bit." Then she casts a steely glance in my direction in case I might blurt out that I hate having somebody else puttering around in my own personal private space.

Anyway, Nora slept around the clock. She just woke long enough to go to the bathroom and take meals. But by Christmas Eve, Nora was really wide awake. After one of Mom's enormous holiday meals — supper seemed to go on forever — we went into the living room and opened our presents. Ten o'clock, Uncle Buck yawned and yawned.

"Time to call it a day," he said, and went off to the sunroom, where he insists upon sleeping whenever he visits. He must have popped right off, because we could hear his snores loud and clear.

Mom had removed Sinbad from the sunroom so he wouldn't disturb Uncle Buck.

"Harvey can sleep through a tornado," Mom tells everyone, but honestly, that's only when I'm really tired. Actually, I'm a light sleeper. I wasn't looking forward to Sinbad's company, since he is one noisy bird. Even the cover on his cage doesn't keep him quiet.

Want an example? This morning, for instance, he started singing almost before the crack of dawn.

Would you believe a bird that greets the day with the "Star-Spangled Banner"? He could be heard all over the house.

>Oh, say can you see,
>By the dawn's early light?

It was like having your brain punctured by a red-hot needle. He ended by screaming, "Up! Up! Everybody! Rise and shine!"

My sister Georgeann popped out of her room just as I was coming out of the bathroom.

"Harvey Willson," she ordered through clenched teeth. "You get down there and shut that . . . that . . . *bird* up this minute."

She flipped her head as though she still had a long thick blond ponytail, forgetting she had massacred her hair. Now it was short and stood up in weird spikes. Believe me, Dracula would faint dead away if they met in the hall.

"Me? How am I supposed to do that?" I wanted to know. "Why don't you ask me to do something easy, like make Niagara Falls fall up instead of down?"

Georgeann glared at me. "I can't think of anything worse than living with an eleven-year-old boy."

"Hang around," I yelled after her as she stormed back to her room. "In another three months I'll be twelve."

Anyway, there we were in the living room that evening, Mom, Dad, Nora, and me. Sinbad had ordered us to freeze. And I was teasing Nora, because she takes everything you say seriously. But now she paid no attention to me. She sank way back in the chair opposite me, her dark eyes wide and solemn in her owl face. She didn't look at me at all, because she couldn't tear her gaze away from Sinbad.

We were used to him because of the many times we visited my uncle Buck. But he was a revelation to Nora.

Just then my dog Butch wandered in from the kitchen. He's big and fat and real old. He's the same age I am, but in dog years Butch is retired.

The minute Sinbad spotted Butch, he

snarled, "OUT!" He sounded exactly like my dad. Poor Butch. His brown eyes got sad and weepy, and he slunk out of the room looking puzzled and guilty at the same time.

"How does Sinbad do that?" Nora wondered. She was fascinated. Well, she would be, of course. Nora loves animals. She even likes snakes.

Nora had asked the right question. My dad never loses a chance to hand out information. He calls it "stretching our minds." He does it even if you don't feel you want to know all that much in the first place. Now, though, he had the perfect listener in Nora.

"The African gray parrot," he began, "is a natural-born talker. He can imitate almost any voice or sound. His imitations are so remarkable that it's often impossible to tell his parrot voice from a human voice."

Nora nodded. "Like just now, when he yelled at Butch."

Sinbad is a real showoff. He acted as if he knew my dad was discussing him. He said, "Joy. Can I have another piece of that apple pie?"

Mom said automatically, "Of course, Uncle Buck," then her face flushed red, and she gave Sinbad an angry look.

"I simply cannot get used to that bird," she muttered.

Mom doesn't really like Sinbad. She has this fixed idea that birds should be small and dainty, like canaries, and sing their little hearts out. That's what she says. Birds should not talk. It just isn't natural, Mom insists. Furthermore, she doesn't like the fact that Sinbad refuses to stay in his cage. He prefers to perch on top of it, and take off when he's in the mood.

Mom says creatures of the wild should live in the wild, and you should not have to duck a bird in the house.

"Tell me more," Nora begged.

Mom and I exchanged horrified looks. Tell her more? There would be no stopping my dad now. If he had slides, he'd have set up the projector and screen in a flash.

"Well, Nora," he began. His smile was so brilliant, I was surprised it didn't blind her. He was one very happy man.

Mom waited it out as long as she could.

Then she covered a huge yawn with her hand and stood up. "I'm exhausted," she said. "I'm off to bed. And I think the rest of you," she gave my dad a piercing glance, "should clear out and let Harvey get some sleep. It's been a long day." She yawned again as she left.

But no one took the hint. The longer my dad droned on, the more delighted Nora was, and the wearier I became. I had heard all the stories about Sinbad, more than once. I looked longingly at the sofabed. I thought about Uncle Buck, snug in the sunroom, and Nora going upstairs to sleep in my comfortable bed.

My sister Georgeann had gone up to her room right after supper. She's going to be in a play in school, so she stands in front of her mirror and studies her lines, and her expressions, and her movements. She used to insist she wanted to be a chef. Now she's decided she has a "calling" — that's what she says — a "calling" to the stage. Sixteen-year-old girls are sure hard to figure out. Maybe she'll change when she's seventeen, but she'll have to move fast, because seventeen is practically right around the corner.

Mom had suggested that Georgeann share her room with Nora. You'd think she'd been asked to share it with the Abominable Snowman.

"I'd rather die!" Georgeann clutched her throat, rolled her eyes, and groaned. I guess maybe she does have a calling for the stage.

Just the same, I could understand how she felt. Nora has visited us before. Somehow things start happening when she's around. But that's not my sister's biggest objection. It's Nora. She's changed. She used to tell the most whopping lies. She'd look you right in the eye with this sincere expression on her face and then make the most ridiculous statement. She still did, but she'd added something new to her routine. Now she also told the truth.

Nora being Nora, it isn't the kind of truth you want to hear. Want an example? Georgeann loathes spiders. This morning, just before breakfast, she had swatted one with a long-handled broom.

"Don't ever do that again," Nora had shouted at her.

"What's your problem?" Georgeann demanded.

"The spider." Nora practically sobbed. "I could hear him screaming."

Georgeann couldn't eat breakfast after that, and I wasn't too keen on eating, myself.

Later Mom explained this was only Nora's way of reacting to the hurt she felt because her parents had gone on a Christmas cruise and sent her off to stay with us.

"Nora is resentful, and upset," Mom said. "She'll grow out of this kind of behavior when she's older. But meanwhile, Georgeann, and especially you, Harvey," Mom warned, sounding like a drill sergeant with a bunch of rookies, "you two be nice to her."

Mom didn't add "or else," but we got the message.

It was easy for Georgeann, when she just stayed up in her room, rehearsing her lines for the play. But Nora cornered her when she came out in the hall the first morning Nora went to the bathroom. Nora stared at Georgeann's hair. Then she said something we all thought but didn't say out loud, "You look like you just escaped from Nightmare Alley." Later she mentioned that Georgeann ought to concentrate on being a chef because she couldn't act her way out of a paper bag.

Well, *I* know that. Mom and Dad know that. Maybe even, secretly, Georgeann knows that. It didn't mean she wanted to *hear* it.

I could have told Nora, there are all kinds of truth, and she picked the worst of the lot. I began to worry about her visit. I even began to hope that Nora would stick to her outrageous lies, and forget about telling the truth.

She wasn't too popular with my mom right now, either, because at suppertime Nora told my mom she was wasteful when she threw out some leftover spinach. People were starving all over the world, Nora informed her, and they'd be grateful for that spinach.

Mom opened her mouth, and closed it, firmly.

I must admit Nora hadn't said a word to me or my dad. She was too interested in hearing about Sinbad. I yawned, a real loud noisy yawn. Then I stretched and stretched, to give Nora a hint. But she wasn't going to budge out of the room while my dad talked about Sinbad. Like I said, Dad will hand out tidbits of information any time. And with Nora gazing wide-eyed at him and hanging on his every word, he wasn't about to quit.

"You see, Nora," Dad told her. "Uncle Buck has had Sinbad a long time. And he has taught Sinbad so many things."

"So did Captain Corbin," I reminded him. They both ignored me.

"How did Uncle Buck get Sinbad?" Nora asked in that eager voice of hers. "Maybe I could get a parrot, too."

I couldn't believe she said that. Nora? Have a bird? In *her* house? Pandemonium wouldn't be a strong enough word to describe how my aunt Mildred would carry on.

My dad paid no attention, just continued, "Uncle Buck had a close friend who was captain of a freighter. Whenever Captain Corbin, as Harvey just mentioned, was in port, he stayed with Buck. Corbin had Sinbad on his ship, but Sinbad got miserably seasick. So Corbin gave him to Buck. Sinbad and Buck took to each other like peanut butter and jelly. They've never been parted since."

"He's so beautiful," Nora whispered.

Now I ask you. Beautiful?

"Nora," I pointed out, "he's gray. All over. Even his face is kind of a grayish white. Okay, he does have a red tail. And he has that awful watery yellow color in his eyes. But he is your basic gray, and gray is not beautiful."

Nora glared at me as if I had just insulted her dearest friend.

"You shouldn't say things like that in front of him. I'm sure he's very sensitive."

Wouldn't you think an eleven-year-old girl would have more sense?

"He's a bird!" I said.

"That doesn't mean he hasn't any feelings," she flashed back.

"We'd better let Harvey get to bed," my dad interfered. "I'm sure he's very sleepy."

"At last!" I muttered.

Dad pulled the sofabed open, and helped me make the bed.

"I'll swap with you, Harvey," Nora offered. "You shouldn't have to give up your room just for me. I don't mind staying down here."

"I wouldn't think of it." See? I can be polite if I have to. She didn't want to be parted from Sinbad, but I wanted to go to sleep right that minute.

Just as Nora began to leave the room, with dragging feet and longing glances back at the cage, Dad said, "By the way, Nora. Remind me to tell you tomorrow about Sinbad's having a clue to a hidden treasure."

Nora's ears perked up. Her eyes glowed. She turned back to stare hopefully at him.

"Secret?" she cried. "Hidden treasure?"

Dad shook his head. "Tomorrow, Nora." He was quite firm about that.

I could hear Nora whispering to herself as she finally left.

"A parrot who has a clue to a hidden treasure! I won't sleep a minute tonight!"

2

In which a
nightmare becomes real

I put out the lights, expecting to be sound
asleep the minute my head hit the pillow.
Instead, I tossed and turned, and my mind
was like a buzz saw. I wished my dad
hadn't mentioned the hidden treasure. There
wouldn't be any peace now, not with Nora's
eyes nearly popping out of her head. I could
just imagine her upstairs at this moment,
sitting up, worrying her lower lip the way
she does when she's thinking, and whispering to herself, "Hidden treasure!"

Maybe I should have let Nora stay awhile
so I could explain. It began with Uncle
Buck's best friend, Captain Corbin. It seems
he hid a treasure somewhere in Uncle Buck's
house. Then he taught Sinbad a clue to the

hiding place. Later, he told Uncle Buck what he'd done.

"Just sat there, grinning at me," Uncle Buck told us afterward. "Said all I had to do was use the right word or phrase and Sinbad would give an answer pointing to where the treasure was hidden."

Of course I wanted to know what the treasure was.

"Wouldn't tell me." I remember how exasperated Uncle Buck had been. "I had it coming, though," he had added, "because we played pranks on each other for years."

"Suppose you find the treasure," I wanted to know. "Do you get to keep it?"

"I do now." Uncle Buck sounded sad. His black eyes dimmed with unshed tears.

"He's gone." Uncle Buck's voice was hoarse. "Lost at sea. He was captain of the freighter *Seven Seas*, you know."

I did know. Uncle Buck had told me often enough. Old people do that, tell you things over and over, and Uncle Buck is sixty-nine, so you can bet I've heard everything about a zillion times.

And he cries a lot. Well, not real crying,

just tears that don't quite spill out of his eyes. Then he takes this big handkerchief that looks like a bandana and blows his nose. Since his nose is rather large, it sounds like a foghorn.

"And he left no kith nor kin," I said, to hurry Uncle Buck along.

Uncle Buck nodded. "So I expect the treasure is mine. Whatever it is. If there is a treasure in the first place. This could have been one of his practical jokes."

I planned to tell Nora all about Captain Corbin and his make-believe treasure in the morning. Otherwise, I knew, she would never give me a minute's peace.

I lay in that sofabed and tried to get comfortable, which is hard to do when a spring is fighting to get through the mattress. I could hear Uncle Buck puttering around in the kitchen. It's a habit of his to wake up around midnight to make himself a cup of tea. In a little while, though, he went back to the sunroom, and the house was so quiet you could hear a spider spinning its web.

For a change, Sinbad was quiet, too. And

though I was positive I'd be up all night, I finally dozed off.

I dreamed I was hovering over a volcano. I could see rivers of boiling lava spilling down the mountainside. In the distance, I could hear the wailing of sirens. They came closer and closer, grew louder and louder. I was puzzled. How could firemen expect to put out a volcano?

I was torn out of that nightmare by a shriek that set every nerve in my body leaping wildly to escape.

"FIRE! FIRE!"

It was Sinbad. He was hopping back and forth in his cage under the cover.

I jumped out of bed, yanked the cover off, and yelled, "You stupid bird! Don't you ever do that again!"

I felt stupefied. I was awake, but I could still hear sirens, so loud they seemed to be right outside our house.

"FIRE!" Sinbad screamed again.

Suddenly I heard a new sound. It came from the kitchen. I started toward the dining room — you have to go through the dining room to get to the kitchen — and stopped short. The dining room was filled with smoke escaping through the kitchen door.

I ran back to the foot of the steps.

"Fire! Mom! Dad! Help! The house is on fire!" My voice could have been heard in five counties.

I will say my parents react quickly. I could hear my dad stampeding along the upstairs hall. I didn't wait. I rushed to the kitchen. When I got there, I was stunned. I don't think there is anything more petrifying than to be that close to tongues of fire leaping and crackling in your very own house.

I raced back to the hall to get the fire extinguisher. By the time I got back to the kitchen, Dad was right behind me. He snatched the extinguisher from my hands and was just about to use it when the kitchen door that leads to the yard was smashed in. The sight of an ax splitting through the door paralyzed us. Before we could say a word, two firemen burst in, dragging a hose.

They stared at my dad, with the fire extinguisher in his hand, and shook their heads.

"Sir, get everyone up and out of the house," one of them ordered as they shot a jet of water at the flames.

Just then my mom walked in, with Nora at her heels. Georgeann was right behind them. Then Uncle Buck popped in from the sun-room. Sinbad flew in from the living room and perched on Uncle Buck's shoulder.

"FIRE!" he bellowed in Uncle Buck's ear. Fortunately, Uncle Buck is a little deaf.

Butch came trembling in, too afraid to stay alone in the living room. He huddled against my mom's legs and kept up a steady low whining while he tried to shake himself to pieces in terror. Butch has been my dog forever and I love him, but he is the world's biggest coward.

Luckily, the fire itself had been confined to the kitchen, but the smoke had billowed into the other rooms, burning our eyes and making us cough. Dad ordered us back to the living room, where we flung open the windows to let in the frigid winter wind. We grabbed coats from the hall closet, and Nora wrapped herself and Butch in my blanket.

Then we sat around and stared at one another grimly.

"My beautiful kitchen," Mom mourned. "Ruined."

"I wonder how the fire got started," Nora said.

At that moment, one of the firemen came in. Mom stared at his wet boots and the mud on the carpet and winced.

He paid no attention. "Lucky for you your neighbor called us in time. We found what caused the fire," he added, holding up a twisted black lump of metal. "Someone left an empty pot on a burner." He started to leave, then turned back. "If you folks have someplace else to spend the night, it would be a good idea to go there. This smoke could be hazardous."

When he left, Uncle Buck clapped his hand across his forehead. He looked stricken. "I did it. I forgot to turn the burner off when I made my tea."

No one said a word, which made Uncle Buck feel even more guilty, for he turned to my mom and pleaded with her to yell at him. "Go on, Joy," he urged her. "I deserve it."

But of course she didn't. When my mom gets mad, she turns to ice. You can feel the cold wave all through the house.

Dad stood up. "I'm going in to assess the damage," he said.

So naturally we all trooped in after him.

The kitchen was an absolute disaster.

Dad shook his head. "Let's not tackle this tonight. We're all tired and overwrought. There's nothing we can do now anyway."

Mom didn't budge. "Yes there is, Thor. I'm not moving one step out of here with my kitchen door smashed to bits and practically inviting a burglar to drop in."

My mom is almost as tall as my dad, with black hair and eyes and what Dad calls olive skin. She's usually soft-spoken, maybe because my dad and Georgeann are bellowers. But right now Mom was almost screaming.

"It's all my fault," Uncle Buck moaned.

Dad and Mom ignored him.

"We have that old wooden screen down in the basement," Mom went on in a more normal voice. "I want it nailed across the doorway. Now!"

"I'll help you, Dad," I volunteered.

"Me, too," Nora put in helpfully.

It took the three of us a little while to sort through the mess in the basement to find the screen. Then we had to clean it because it was filthy with dust. I have to admit Nora worked as hard as we did. Of course, she did tell my dad she'd seen pigsties that were cleaner, which made her real popular with both of us.

When we got back upstairs, Dad hammered the screen in place over the kitchen doorway. While he worked, Uncle Buck made an announcement.

"Until all the necessary repairs have been made in the kitchen, and wherever there has been smoke damage in the house, you are all coming to stay with me. There's plenty of room for everyone, including Butch."

Good old Butch. When he heard his name, he thumped his tail and made a sound he probably thought was a bark.

Mom looked at Dad. She expected him to dig in his heels and refuse Uncle Buck's offer immediately. My dad is not one for any kind of a change. He doesn't mind taking a trip, but only if he can be back in his own bed the same night. But he surprised all of us, just took a couple of deep breaths, and nodded.

I happened to glance over at Nora just then. Her eyes were dancing. I could almost hear what she was thinking. We were actually moving to Uncle Buck's house. She'd be right there! On the spot!

And if there was a hidden treasure, she sure expected to be the one to find it.

3

In which there
are some secrets

"This is some weird place," Nora said the next morning. She took in the whole room in one sweeping glance. "I've never been in a kitchen like this."

I believed her. Nobody has kitchens like Uncle Buck's anymore. For one thing, it's an enormous room, with cabinets that don't quit. I mean they march around the walls on three sides. All of them have glass doors, so everything inside is on display. A huge round table that can seat ten people is smack in the middle of the room.

Mom says she's seen ballrooms that were smaller. That isn't a lie, you understand. It's just exaggeration. She doesn't expect you to believe her.

What I like most are the windows in the fourth wall. They crank open; below is a river that flows past quickly, then narrows and disappears around a bend. A path from the back of the house leads down to a boat-house and a small wooden landing.

"Where is everybody?" Nora asked.

I had a mouthful of pancakes drowned in maple syrup, so I didn't answer. Butch was as close as he could get to my chair, quivering with hope, his eyes fixed on every forkful of food.

Just then Myrtle Crump, who was at the stove with her back toward us, turned around.

"The Judge and his missis went to check on the house," she spoke up. "The girl scooted out with her things to go stay with a friend. She mentioned something about having to study lines for some play. And Buck is in the sun parlor reading the obituaries to see which one of his friends has died."

Nora's mouth dropped open. She hadn't met Myrtle Crump yet. I could understand how Nora felt. Myrtle Crump affects people that way when they see her for the first time.

She is over six feet tall and all muscle. She has restless electric-blue eyes, a wild orange-red wig, and bright patches of orange rouge on her cheeks. She wears orange stockings and shoes no matter what color her dresses are. So naturally I always called her the orange lady.

My mom says Myrtle Crump's dresses are called muumuus. When I was little, I used to think that meant Myrtle Crump came from one of those islands that sit out in the Pacific Ocean.

Myrtle Crump loves jewelry. From where I sat it seemed she was wearing all the beads and chains she owns. Long massive earrings with bells in them hung from her large pierced earlobes. It's a wonder her ears didn't sag down to her shoulders. She also wore rings on every finger except her thumbs. When she moved, she rang and clanked. One nice thing about that is you always know when she's coming. There is no way Myrtle Crump could ever sneak up on anybody.

"You're the one they call Nora, I take it." Myrtle Crump slapped a dish of pancakes down on the table. "Eat up, girl. I haven't got all day."

Nora shook her head. "There must be a thousand calories in this food."

Myrtle Crump tipped her head sideways, and glared down at Nora. "You want to count calories, count them. I cook what I cook, and you eat it or do without. It's all the same to me. Stack the dishes when you're through."

She clanked out of the kitchen, and in a second we could hear her in the sun parlor talking to Uncle Buck.

Nora shook her head. "*She's* Uncle Buck's housekeeper? How come? She must know something awful about him . . ."

"About Uncle Buck?" I laughed. "Some deep, dark secret?"

She came back at me impatiently. "Harvey, nobody would have her around the house unless he had to."

"Captain Corbin brought her one day, when Uncle Buck mentioned he needed a housekeeper. It was one of his practical jokes. Only Uncle Buck fooled him and

hired her. That was umpteen years ago . . ."
I noticed she hadn't touched her pancakes.
"Aren't you going to eat them?"

Nora glanced over at Butch. That was
enough. Greed sure makes that dog psychic.
For a slow-moving animal, he can move with
the speed of light where food is concerned.
He was at her side, nudging her so hard he
almost pushed her off her chair. Naturally,
with the way Nora feels about animals, she
gave him most of the pancakes. Of course
she didn't know Butch had already been fed
by Myrtle Crump.

Butch wasn't going to let on; neither was I.

The pancakes disappeared as if by magic
— now you saw them; now you didn't. Then
he looked up at her prayerfully, with his soft
brown eyes telling her she was his last hope.
I don't know how dogs get away with that.

Nora ignored him now. She turned to
me and demanded, "Is this house for real? I
walked around upstairs before I came down.
Did you know there are seven bedrooms?
But only two bathrooms?" She wrinkled her
nose. "Did you see those bathrooms? You
know there are no showers? Only those big,

ugly bathtubs that stand up on claw feet?
And you have to pull a *chain* to flush the
toilet!"

She was outraged.

"I get the message," I yelled.

I suppose I ought to explain something.
Nora's mother and my father are sister and
brother. Uncle Buck is on my mother's side
of the family, and Nora hadn't come in contact with that part of my family, especially
since she lives so far away. So I decided I'd
better tell her about this house.

"Listen," I began, "this place is very old.
It's been in the family since before the Civil
War." I was just about to give her a little
history lesson when she interrupted.

"I know about the Civil War, Harvey.
Don't start getting that superior look of yours
when you think you know something I don't
know."

That got my back up. Here I was, being
nice to her, just like my mom ordered. But
you just can't be nice to some people.

"Do you want to hear this or not?" I didn't
wait for an answer. "People up north used
to help runaway slaves get to Canada." I

spoke rapidly to keep her from interrupting me again. "They set up a system called the Underground Railroad. The houses the runaways stopped at until they could reach Canada were called stations. This was one of the stations."

I gave her a smug smile. Not everybody gets to stay in a house that was part of the country's history.

Nora was awed. I could tell. Just the same, being Nora, she said, "You're probably making all this up. I didn't see any place upstairs where people could hide." She glanced around the kitchen. "Or in here, either."

"Don't be dumb, Nora. Where would you hide people?" I answered my own question. "In a secret hiding place, of course. There's a hidden room, and a secret passage and stairway, and two underground tunnels. One leads out to the meadow. The other leads to the boathouse down at the river."

Nora's eyes opened wide. She was so excited, she almost stuttered when she spoke. "Honestly, Harvey? Really and truly a hidden room and a secret passage?"

Suddenly she leaped up from the table,

grabbed the dishes, and slapped them down in the sink. Then she yanked my arm.

"Prove it, Harvey. I dare you," she challenged. "If you know where they are, show me!"

Of course I knew where they were. Uncle Buck had always encouraged me and Georgeann to explore the house whenever we visited. It used to be scary, but fun, especially on dark, rainy days.

I was just about to take Nora on a tour when we heard Myrtle Crump talking to Sinbad in the living room. What's more, Sinbad was talking, too.

There was no way Nora could resist that. She ran out of the kitchen, tore through the dining room, and into the living room, with me right behind her. I could hear Butch gasping as he tried to keep up with us.

Myrtle Crump was glaring up at Sinbad, who was doing tricks on a trapeze bar Uncle Buck had suspended from the ceiling. He hung upside down and whistled.

It was plain to see Myrtle Crump was exasperated. She had a large book in her hand, which was open to the middle.

"What's going on?" I asked. "Are you reading to him? Are you teaching Sinbad more words?"

She glared at me. "Teach the creature *more* words? He knows too many already. I am trying to get him to give me the clue to the treasure."

Nora's ears stood at attention. She forgot about hidden passages and runaway slaves. Her eyes gleamed. "So there really is a treasure. Harvey tried to make me believe it didn't exist."

Myrtle Crump gave a scornful sniff. "Of course there is a treasure. There has to be. But this stubborn, good-for-nothing bird refuses to cooperate." The look she gave Sinbad made me think he was pushing his luck. "I've tried everything. I've read to him from the dictionary. I've told him fairy tales. I've sung songs. If Captain Corbin was in this room right now, I'd . . . I'd . . ." She caught the expression on our faces and added lamely, "I'd make him tell me."

She wheeled around when Uncle Buck spoke up behind her. He had his paper folded under his arm. His face was one big grin.

"His last practical joke. And his best," Uncle Buck told her. "My friend Corbin's had the last laugh."

"Not yet he hasn't. Not while I'm here," she snapped back. "I thought you were going to stay out in the sun parlor for a while."

"It got to be too gloomy, especially since it's started to rain real hard."

Nora stood there, yearning up at Sinbad, probably trying to figure a way to get him to come perch on her shoulder. I didn't think she heard a word that Uncle Buck said. But she had, for she said, almost automatically,

"Rain, rain, go away,
Come again another day."

Sinbad turned right side up. He peered down at Nora. Then he said, "Every cloud has a silver lining."

It was as if lightning had struck, and lit up my brain with a blinding flash of inspiration.

"Every cloud has a silver lining," I repeated. "Of course. That's it! That's the clue!"

4

In which
a mystery deepens

Uncle Buck was the first to speak. I could tell he didn't know whether to laugh or be angry. He was a little of both when he said, "Harvey, I am sick and tired of hearing about this so-called treasure. A joke is a joke, but this one has gone too far."

I guess my expression — deep disappointment mixed with some resentment — bothered him.

He grinned and slapped me lightly on my shoulder.

"Never mind. It's raining. That makes it a good day for fun and games. What's this wonderful clue of yours?"

Sinbad chose this moment to add his penny's worth.

"Harvey!" he scolded, sounding just like my mom when she's finally lost all patience with me. "Grow up, Harvey!"

He gave a maniacal laugh straight out of a horror show.

Myrtle Crump's mouth had fallen open when I shouted, "That's the clue!" Now she grabbed my arm and shook me. "Don't just stand there. Explain."

Nora found her voice, too. "Well? Is there a clue? Are you going to tell us or just tease us?"

I took a deep breath. "Uncle Buck, you still keep everything the same in Captain Corbin's old room, don't you?"

He stared at me as if he'd heard a lot of dumb questions but never one as stupid as this.

"You know I do, Harvey. Why wouldn't I?"

Of course I knew that. Uncle Buck hadn't touched anything in the room since he got the news that Captain Corbin had been lost at sea. Myrtle Crump cleaned it, and searched every nook and cranny for the treasure as well, I bet.

I'm not sure what a nook is and I wouldn't know a cranny if it bit me. That's just one of Myrtle Crump's expressions. "I've cleaned every nook and cranny in this house," I've heard her tell Uncle Buck once in a while.

Whenever I peeked in the room, it seemed to me it had a waiting look, as if Captain Corbin might just walk in one day.

"Of course he won't," Mom had explained. "But Uncle Buck just won't let go."

"All his clothes and everything?" I persisted. After all, Mom had mentioned that quite a while back, so I wanted to make sure nothing had changed Uncle Buck's mind.

Myrtle Crump shook me again, setting her bells jangling and her bracelets clanging.

"Talk!" she exploded.

So I talked.

"You remember that warm quilted mandarin robe Captain Corbin brought back from China? The one that was red silk, with clouds and dragons and what all embroidered all over it?"

"Clouds," Nora repeated softly.

I ignored her. "You remember the lining, Uncle Buck? It was sort of a gray silvery color."

I folded my arms and smiled triumphantly. I narrowed my eyes. I nodded my head wisely.

"Every cloud has a silver lining," I said, spacing out the words.

"A clue if I ever heard one. Let's go." Myrtle Crump was halfway out of the room when Uncle Buck called her back. She turned in surprise.

"I just thought of something," he told her. "You remember the door we used to have between the sun parlor and the living room?" He didn't wait for an answer. "The Judge could use it in his kitchen. I want you to help me bring that door up from the basement. Then we'll drive over. . ."

"But it would only take a minute for me to run upstairs," she pleaded with him.

"If there's a treasure up there, it can wait till we get back. If it's waited this long, another hour or so won't matter." To soften the blow, he added, "Let the kids search for it. They've nothing better to do anyway." He headed for the basement. I offered to help, but he waved me aside. "Myrtle can do it."

Myrtle Crump was torn. She desperately wanted to find the treasure, but she had to give Uncle Buck a hand. He'd never manage that door by himself.

When they came up again, with Myrtle Crump clutching the door, and Uncle Buck holding it at one edge, they started out the front hall.

Myrtle Crump took a minute to yell back at me, "You bring that robe downstairs and wait till we get back. No matter how long it takes, hear."

The minute they were gone, Nora and I raced upstairs. She didn't know which room it was, so she had to follow, but she was so close on my heels, I could feel her breath on the back of my neck.

Doors lined both sides of a long, rather narrow hallway. Just as we passed the last bedroom, the hall made a sharp right turn. If you weren't familiar with the house, you might not even know there was an additional room.

I opened the door and started to go in when I noticed that Nora was hanging back.

"What's the matter?" I asked impatiently.

"I've never been in a dead man's room before."

"Girls!" I muttered. "Nobody *died* in this room."

She gave me one of her lofty looks. "Girls are sensitive. They can *sense* things, Harvey. They have feelings boys don't know anything about. Like the feeling I have right now," she added.

"Terrific." I shook my head. "Now you're going to pull some psychic stuff on me, right?"

She pressed her fingers against her forehead. "I see the ghost of Captain Corbin. He's beckoning to us, Harvey. From his watery grave, he's warning us."

I knew it was an act, but it made me feel uncomfortable.

"You can stay out here if you want to. I'm going in." I didn't wait to see if she was following. I knew curiosity would bring her in a hurry.

Everything was just as I remembered. A

clock set in a steering wheel was still ticking. That tick-tock, tick-tock shattered the quiet. Above a long mahogany dresser, a scimitar with a wicked curve decorated the wall. On the dresser was a statue of an Indian god. It was painted white, with a blue neck, and it had three eyes. A garland made up of skulls hung round its throat. A large snake wound itself around the statue's neck. And it had four hands.

I thought Nora's eyes would pop out of her head when she saw it.

"Captain Corbin brought that back from India," I told her. But she wasn't listening. She had caught sight of a model of a sailing ship on the wide headboard behind the bed.

Her eyes glowed, the way they do when she's surprised, or happy. "That's beautiful." She didn't say the words: she breathed them, as if a loud sound might wreck the ship.

"It's okay," I said. Well, after all, I'd seen that ship lots of times. To tell you the truth, I'd rather look at a space capsule. I thought I ought to explain about the ship to Nora. "Captain Corbin made that."

"He didn't!" she exclaimed.

Now why do people do that? I just said he did, didn't I?

"That was his hobby. On those long, boring trips in the freighter, he made lots of ships. All sizes. Then he stuck them in bottles. I never could figure out why anyone would want to do that," I went on. "But Uncle Buck went wild over them. He has a glass cabinet full of them on display in his room."

I didn't add that I couldn't understand why Uncle Buck was so enthusiastic about them. When you've seen one, you've seen them all, as far as I'm concerned.

"Would you like to see them?" I offered, remembering my mom's instructions to be polite to Nora. But her eye had been caught by a helmet on the floor next to the dresser. It was one used by an undersea diver — large, heavy, and forbidding. It gave me the shivers every time I saw it.

Nora hunched her shoulders, as if a chill wind had touched her. I felt the same way, but why? Everything was exactly as I remembered it, but somehow today it seemed different.

Nora is sure sensitive to other people's

moods. She caught me up on it right away.

"What is it, Harvey? Something's wrong in here and you know it, don't you?"

"Cut that out," I ordered. But she was right. I was uneasy, but I didn't know why.

Suddenly Nora whipped her head right, then left.

"I smell something, Harvey."

"All closed-up rooms get a musty odor," I told her.

When she shook her head, I sniffed. Once. Twice.

"Tobacco smoke. As if someone smoked a pipe in here," I whispered.

Nora edged toward the door. I felt like doing the same. Why was I suddenly sure someone had been in the room only minutes before we arrived? Then I laughed with relief.

"My dad must have come in here and looked around. I'll bet he had his pipe."

I could visualize him puffing away as he studied the room, wondering when Uncle Buck would finally accept the fact that Jack Corbin was gone.

"Oh," Nora said. She sounded let down. Tell her a house has a secret passage and a hidden room and she's ready for a real spooky adventure.

"Can we look for the robe now?" I asked sarcastically. "Or are you going to pull off another act?"

She ignored my comment.

"What's that?" She pointed to an enormous old-fashioned wardrobe against the back wall. It had two massive wooden doors with a large, elaborate lock that was obviously broken. The wardrobe was made of mahogany and had a deep reddish brown luster. The whole thing was carved with intricate designs from top to bottom. At the base, there were heavy claw feet that rested solidly on the bare wood floor.

"That is the ugliest piece of furniture I ever saw in my entire life," Nora said. "I wouldn't sleep in the same room with that if I was paid to do it." Before I could utter a word, she went on, "*Things* could hide in there." She lowered her voice and began to weave her hands in the air. "Just imagine, Harvey. It's late at night. Everything is dark. Slowly . . . silently . . . the doors swing open and then — *whoosh!*"

I snapped my head around to stare at her,
then turned back to study the wardrobe. Were
the doors opening, little by little? What with
the rain pelting the window, and the gloom
of the day creating odd shadows in the room,
and Nora whispering in that eerie voice, I
felt spooked.

So naturally I got mad and yelled at her.

"You and your imagination. If you're
scared, why don't you leave? Nobody ex-
pects a girl to be brave," I added. I knew that
would get her back up for sure.

She gave me a fiery look that was supposed
to reduce me to ashes, then she marched to
the wardrobe, flung open the doors, and
studied the clothes hanging there.

"Well, Harvey," she asked finally,
"where's this wonderful robe you were talking about?"

I pushed her aside and went through the
clothes carefully.

Then I turned to Nora, and I knew I must
have looked as pale as I felt.

The mandarin robe was gone!

5

In which there are shadows from the past

"It isn't here!" My tone was one of total disbelief. And why wouldn't it be? Everything else still looked the same; all of Captain Corbin's other clothes still hung in the wardrobe, just as he had left them.

So why would the mandarin robe be missing?

"It doesn't make sense," I went on. "That robe should be here."

Nora made an impatient clicking sound. "Don't be so dumb, Harvey. Don't you see what's happened? Somebody else got that same clue from Sinbad."

"If we're talking dumb," I shot back at her, "then that's dumb with a capital *D*. Nobody in this house got that clue till I did. Uncle

Buck and Myrtle Crump went to help my mom and dad. That leaves you and me."

Nora's eyes grew big and round. "We should have brought Butch with us for protection."

"*Butch?* To begin with, he can't get up the steps. For another thing, that dog is afraid of his own shadow. And if he had to attack someone, he'd probably fall asleep while he was doing it."

Nora shivered. "Well, somebody must have been in this room." She glanced around as if she expected Captain Corbin's ghost to materialize.

"There's a perfectly simple explanation," I began. There had to be. For one thing, I had seen that robe the last time we visited. I even asked if I could try it on, but Uncle Buck didn't go for that at all.

"Jack didn't like people to touch his things." Uncle Buck's voice was severe. And my mom frowned and shook her head at me.

"Of course," I said. "I know what happened. It probably fell to the bottom of the wardrobe. Just slipped off the hanger."

"Of course," Nora echoed with relief.

I climbed into the wardrobe, with Nora right behind me. I knew she was anxious to grab the robe first. She rubbed her arms up and down. I felt the chill as well. Dank, moist air seemed to be rising from the bottom and back of the wardrobe.

"Where's that cold air coming from?" Nora wondered. She sounded subdued. I think just then she wanted to climb out, run to her bedroom, pop into bed, and yank a blanket over her head. "It must be Captain Corbin's aura or something." When I shook my head at her, she went on. "People have auras, Harvey. I see them all the time." She lowered her voice. "I can see yours now. Strange things will happen to you soon."

I wished she wouldn't keep making me feel so uneasy. I don't believe all that aura stuff, but she almost had me believing her. Just the same, I have a stubborn streak. I came looking for that mandarin robe, and I wasn't going to leave without it.

I held my hand in the air and traced that flow of air to the center of the wardrobe's back wall. And I knew instantly what had happened. Nora didn't know it, but there was

a secret door at the back of the wardrobe.
Now, as my hand went through that current
of air, it touched the door, which was partially ajar. I pushed, and the door opened
smoothly and silently.

That bothered me. After all the time that
had gone by, why hadn't the door creaked?

Nora gasped. She came closer and peered
beyond the open door.

"Harvey!" She kept her voice low, as if
afraid she might be overheard. "Look! Steps!
They must lead down to that hidden room
you told me about."

I couldn't see her clearly, but I had a feeling her eyes had begun to shine. She might
be scared, but there was no way she could
resist a secret stairway leading to a hidden
room. Even the weather — gloomy and over-
cast and bone-chilling — was just right.

I wasn't too keen on carrying this search
on anymore. There was something wrong.
It was just a hunch. But sometimes hunches
are warnings. So I objected. "That's a real
twisty stairway. And it's dark. Very dark."

"Oh Harvey. Come on. Let's explore! You

have that key flashlight of yours in your pocket. We could use that."

She was ready to go down that stairway whether I came along or not. I wasn't going to let a cousin — a *girl* cousin — make me look afraid. So I pulled the flashlight from my pocket, tested it to see if it still worked, and insisted that I go first.

The light was so dim, it surprised me to notice how large and threatening our shadows loomed on the wall.

The air was frigid, raising goose bumps up and down my arms. I could even see Nora's breath when she spoke.

"Can't you just feel the presence of those runaways?" she whispered as we inched our way down the steps. "Scared. And worried. Hanging on to their few belongings. Wanting to look back over their shoulders all the time."

I glanced quickly at our shadows on the wall. Now they seemed to be joined by the shadows of the runaways. It made me wonder if all their shadows were imprinted there.

Feeling my way downward, I thought

about all those runaways. Had they stolen down in grim silence, terrified they might still be caught, uncertain and fearful of what lay ahead?

I hoped everyone who had come to this house had made it to freedom.

Uncle Buck had once mentioned the idea of selling the house. It was too big, he said. And he was old. But here on this stairway, I knew Uncle Buck could never let the house go. It was too much a part of living history.

The stairway wound itself down into an open doorway, to a room we could hardly see in the thin ray of the flashlight.

"There used to be a hurricane lamp on that table in the middle of the room," I told Nora. "I know there's a candle in it. Maybe there are still some matches there, too."

I eased my way across the room carefully, with Nora clutching my shoulder, until we reached the table. I pointed the light down.

"Look, Harvey," Nora cried. "Someone carved some letters here. She traced them with her finger, then read aloud.

Free at last   Aaron 1859

I couldn't speak. I must have seen those
words carved in the table when I explored
the house with Georgeann. I had been too
little then to understand. Now I knew what
they meant.

"Harvey, I can't tell." Nora poked me.
"Are there matches anywhere? If you can
light the lamp, we might be able to see if anything else is carved on the table. Or if there's
writing on the walls."

I reached over and carefully removed the
glass chimney. Then I stood absolutely still.

Nora must have felt all the radiations I
sent out.

"What is it, Harvey?" She glanced around
nervously. "What's wrong?"

I spoke so softly, she had to lean in close
to hear me.

"Somebody has been here. And not too
long ago," I told her.

She was stunned. "Here? In this room?
How do you know?"

"The lamp," I said. "The glass chimney
is still warm."

6

In which
a stranger appears

We stared at each other. I felt as scared as
Nora looked. Well, I ask you. Wouldn't you
get goose bumps all over if you discovered
that someone, or some*thing*, had been right
in this room, just minutes before you arrived?
I knew, with certainty, that someone, or
something, had climbed the dark stairway to
the wardrobe, and had left the secret door
ajar.

I admit my goose bumps felt the size of
baseballs when I realized that he — or it —
was wandering around the house now.

It was obvious Nora had the same thought,
for she turned and glanced apprehensively
toward the stairway. "Is there another way
out?" she asked hopefully.

I nodded. "There's the tunnel. We can follow it to the boathouse. Or we can veer off when it turns and go to the meadow."

"Are there lights in the tunnel, Harvey?"

When I shook my head, Nora said firmly, "No way am I walking through a dark tunnel to a boathouse where somebody is lurking."

I wished she hadn't used that word. *Lurking* immediately drew a vivid picture in my mind of some evil creature hiding in the shadows of the boathouse, ready to leap out at us. The way my imagination was working overtime, I didn't need Nora to continue, but she did.

"Suppose whoever was here is there? He could be a dangerous criminal. He could capture us and hold us for ransom. We might never see our loved ones again." Nora was so interested in her own words, she couldn't seem to stop. "He might have a boat. He might kidnap us, and take us to China, and . . ."

"*Kidnap* us?" I interrupted. "*China?*" I had had enough. I marched to the door.

"Where are you going," she yelled at me.

"Upstairs." My voice was steady, though my insides felt like Jell-O. "It's freezing down here." That was true enough. My teeth were chattering, and it wasn't all because of fear.

Nora was glad I had made the decision. She followed me upstairs without another word.

When we got back into the wardrobe, I made sure the secret door was shut tight. Then I walked quickly down the hall to the stairway, with Nora close as my shadow. We were almost all the way down when I stopped so abruptly that Nora nearly knocked me over. I held my finger to my lips.

"Shhhh!" I hissed as she seemed about to speak. Then I hung over the banister and listened hard.

"It's only Uncle Buck and Myrtle Crump." Nora kept her voice low.

I shushed her again. Now she could hear it, too. Someone else was in the living room with them. We could hear the rise and fall of a man's voice.

"The man who was in the hidden room!" Nora exclaimed.

If they gave prizes for people who jump to conclusions, Nora would win by a mile. We didn't know who had been in that room. Nor did we have any idea who Uncle Buck's visitor was. I told Nora that.

"There's only one way to find out," she replied, and went past me. This time I had to follow her lead. We skidded to a stop just before we came to the living room. Suddenly, Nora turned shy. She held me back.

"Let's just peek in first," she suggested.

I shrugged. Sometimes it's easier to go along with Nora than argue. So we hid partially behind the door and peered into the room.

Uncle Buck and Myrtle Crump faced away from us. That gave Nora and me a clear view of the man standing before them. He was tall and slender. His face, long and narrow, seemed to come to a point in a short black beard. His black mustache was hard to see because he kept running his thumb and forefinger over it as he spoke. What impressed me at once were his eyes. They were quite large, a remarkable deep brown that seemed luminous, as if reflecting light.

Though he wore a gray suit, with a vest, and a black-and-gray tie, and black shoes, his head was wrapped in a white turban.

We couldn't quite hear what he was saying, but his words had a lilt that made Nora's eyes glow.

"He's an Indian," I told her. "From India," I added, in case Nora misunderstood.

Nora didn't care. She was so fascinated that before I knew it, she burst into the living room. Once again, I had to follow.

"Come in. Come in," Uncle Buck invited us. "I want you to meet Mr. Ranvir Singh. He was a close personal friend of Captain Corbin."

Myrtle Crump frowned at me. "Say hello," she ordered.

I was tempted to tell her that I was eleven going on twelve and I knew how to say hello without being told. But I could see Myrtle Crump was so dazzled that she didn't know whether she was coming or going. Her eyes were glued to Mr. Singh's face, and she hung on his every word as if each one was a precious jewel. She was quivering all over,

which set her bells to ringing and her bracelets to clanging.

And Nora! She stood as if turned to stone.
I couldn't believe it! I glanced from her to
Myrtle Crump and back again. They were
in love! Can you tie that? Just because the
stranger was handsomer than a movie star,
was that any reason to go bananas? I'm not
bad-looking myself, if you want to know, but
not a single solitary girl has ever fainted because I walked into a room.

"How do you do, Mr. Singh?" I asked.
Too bad Georgeann wasn't around to hear
how politely I asked. She claims a baboon has
better manners than I have, and she tells my
mom over and over that I am a constant em-
barrassment to her.

"I am most well, thank you," Mr. Singh
said.

"You guys came back kind of fast," I told
Uncle Buck. "How come?"

Myrtle Crump pointed to several card-
board boxes crammed full of stuff. "The
Judge wanted his own pillows, and your mom
had to have her own blanket. And we have

to have extra bed linens for everybody, plus bathrobes, and slippers, and clothes . . ."

I held up my hand. "I get the idea."

You ask a simple question and you get an inventory!

"We're going back to help clean up. Things are in a terrible mess over there," Myrtle Crump went on.

That's what she said, but it seemed to me she wasn't planning on moving in a hurry now, or ever. Tear herself away from the handsomest man she had ever been this close to in her entire life? Not likely.

Mr. Singh coughed — a small, polite cough — to remind everyone he was still in the room. I turned to him and pointed to his turban. "Are you a Sikh?"

I pronounced it "sick."

"Harvey," Nora gasped. "That's rude."

"Not at all, my dear young lady," Mr. Singh assured her. He smiled at me. I was surprised that some of his teeth were crooked. You'd expect everything about him to be perfect. "It is spelled S-i-k-h but pronounced 'seek.' It is my religion."

"I know," I said, and I sent Nora a significant look, so she would notice how much smarter than she is I am and always have been. "You have long black hair under the turban, right?"

Mr. Singh nodded.

"Mr. Singh was just telling us about Jack — Captain Corbin," Uncle Buck said. He sounded hoarse, as if he had swallowed a lot of tears.

"I brought so sad news," Mr. Singh explained. "That the good captain, whom I cherished, died in my arms."

That made me feel real bad. Somehow, because Uncle Buck wouldn't accept Captain Corbin's death, I had had a notion in the back of my mind that maybe he would show up some day. One look at Uncle Buck's face told me that Mr. Singh had destroyed all of Uncle Buck's last lingering hopes.

"He gave me this ring and asked that I place it personally in your hands." Mr. Singh continued talking to Uncle Buck.

He worked a large gold ring from the middle finger of his right hand. The ring had a curious design, two snakes intertwined, with one having ruby eyes, the other eyes of green jade.

"You recognize it?" Mr. Singh asked softly.

Uncle Buck took it without a word, just the slightest nod of his head. But I noticed that he stared at the ring and then at Mr. Singh, and his lips tightened.

Mr. Singh had turned away, his attention now focused on Sinbad, who had been unusually quiet up to now. Suddenly, he squawked, "Birds of a feather flock together."

Mr. Singh's head jerked up. He studied Sinbad with his remarkable eyes. Then he turned back to Uncle Buck. "You will forgive me if I ask a personal question. The treasure. Have you discovered it yet?"

"I knew it," Myrtle Crump shouted. She shot a triumphant glare at Uncle Buck. "*Now* do you believe there's a treasure? And Sinbad does have the clue."

"Indeed, yes, dear madam. The bird has the clue. The problem, no doubt, is to wrest it from him?"

"But Harvey already got the clue," Nora blurted out. "Only we couldn't find the robe."

I was furious. "Girls," I practically hissed in her ear. "Blabbermouths!"

"I didn't know it was a secret," she flashed back at me impatiently. "Anyway, since the robe is missing, what difference does it make?"

"Missing?" Uncle Buck repeated. "What do you mean, missing?"

Mr. Singh interrupted smoothly. He held up his hand and waved the idea away. "No clue at all, young fellow. Captain Corbin was too clever by far to leave so simple a clue. So the missing robe is of little importance."

Nora made a face at me. I guess she'd been annoyed all along that I was the one who had thought of the clue in the first place.

Just then the phone rang. I was closest, so I answered. It was my mom. She wanted Myrtle Crump to bring a pile of rags back with her, and my uncle was not to forget the extra garbage pails and liners that Mom needed, and could they please hurry.

I relayed the message.

As Myrtle Crump tore herself away with

a sigh so deep I expected the carpet to rise clear off the floor, Uncle Buck said, "You kids want to come along, or stay here?"

Nora whispered, with a soulful glance at Mr. Singh, "We'll stay."

Do girls know how sappy they sound when they have a crush on somebody? Boys have more sense. Of course, I did once have a crush on Karen Bluethorpe, but she used to pass me by like she was the queen bee and I was just another drone, so I gave her up.

Uncle Buck turned to Mr. Singh. He seemed to study him closely for a moment, but when he spoke, Uncle Buck sounded very hospitable. "Listen, any friend of Jack Corbin's is a friend of mine. Please be our guest while you are here," he urged. "Harvey will show you to one of the bedrooms. Myrtle and I should be back in a little while. Then we can have a good, long talk. Of course you'll stay for dinner this evening."

Mr. Singh made a small bow. "You are most gracious."

When Uncle Buck and Myrtle Crump left, I asked Mr. Singh, "Would you like to come upstairs now and rest?"

"You are most thoughtful, young man. But if I might just sit here while you prepare the room?"

I shrugged. "Sure. Why not?" I yanked Nora's arm and dragged her with me. "I need help."

As soon as we were out of earshot, she said angrily, "What's the matter with you anyway, Harvey? Why couldn't I stay and talk to him?"

"I have something to tell you." I walked to the first step and made believe I was going up the stairway. Nora followed, most unwillingly. I glanced back and noticed that Mr. Singh had come to the door to see if I was really on the way up. I smiled, and he smiled back. Then he disappeared back into the living room.

"Okay, Harvey. What's eating you?"

"I don't trust him, that's what."

Nora stared at me as if I had suddenly gone berserk. Not trust Mr. Singh? her expression said. Not trust the most beautiful person she had ever seen in her life?

"The ring," I went on, still in a low urgent whisper. "Uncle Buck told me Captain Corbin would never part with it. Captain Corbin wanted to be buried with it, because it was given to him by his sweetheart, who died before they could be married."

"Then why didn't your Uncle Buck say something? Why did he ask him to stay?" she asked.

I shrugged. "How should I know? Maybe he's forgotten. Maybe hearing that Captain Corbin is really dead was too much of a shock for him to remember."

"That's so sad, about the ring." Nora sighed. She didn't know whether to be touched to the heart by such a sentimental story, or put her faith in Mr. Singh. The romantic tale won out, of course.

"What shall we do?" she wanted to know.

I tiptoed back down the steps, motioning her to be quiet. Then we peered into the room.

Mr. Singh stood in front of Sinbad, who cocked his head, and then said again, loud and clear, "Birds of a feather flock together."

"So that's the clue," Mr. Singh purred. He turned and let his gaze cover the room from wall to wall. Then he froze.

We followed his glance. I let out a deep breath. Nora did, too.

"So that's the real clue," she whispered. She sounded upset, and I didn't blame her. It didn't seem fair that a perfect stranger should be the one to find the treasure.

Mr. Singh walked directly to the doorway that led to the sunroom. On each side of the doorway were two large vases. They rose about three feet from the floor. In each vase was a huge display of peacock feathers.

"Birds of a feather," Mr. Singh said aloud. He had a triumphant air about him.

"Why doesn't Butch get up and bite him?" Nora demanded.

That was when I realized for the first time that Butch was half sitting beside Sinbad's cage, watching every move Mr. Singh made.

"Butch? Bite somebody? We're lucky if he remembers to growl," I complained.

Mr. Singh had removed the feathers and placed them carefully on the floor. Then he upended the vases, one at a time. Nora clasped her hands together so tightly her knuckles rose like small peaks. My hands were clenched into fists. As soon as Mr. Singh laid one finger on the treasure, I was set to go in and . . .

Nora clamped a hand over her mouth to keep from shrieking.

There was no treasure!

Mr. Singh turned back, to glare at Sinbad. Then he nodded his head, as if he had come to a decision, reached into one of his pockets, and pulled out a shiny object. It seemed to be a silver medallion; inside the medallion a silver spiral twisted and turned.

Sinbad stared at it with unblinking eyes. Even Butch was fascinated.

Mr. Singh swung the medallion back and forth, back and forth. As he did so, he spoke in a soft, monotonous voice.

Nora gasped, and grabbed my arm.

"Harvey!" she cried. "He's trying to hypnotize Sinbad!"

7

In which Sinbad
reveals a clue

Mr. Singh finally stopped swinging the silver medallion. Glancing about quickly, he slipped it back into his pocket. Then he spoke.

"I command you to give me the clue to the treasure."

Sinbad was motionless. When Sinbad didn't respond immediately, Mr. Singh repeated his command. And still Sinbad remained stubbornly quiet.

I noticed how Mr. Singh's hands, which now hung down at each side, clenched and unclenched. I guess he was nervous. After all, he had no idea when Uncle Buck and Myrtle Crump might return, or even if Nora and I might pop in. He radiated such waves of tension I could almost reach out and touch them.

"Pay attention, you mangy, moth-eaten excuse for a bird," Mr. Singh suddenly shouted.

Nora and I stared at one another. What happened to that special singsong way Indians speak? Or the softness of the voice, which I personally think is kind of nice? The same man stood there, but it was as if someone else had taken him over.

"I am Captain Corbin. You remember me, Sinbad. Be a good fellow," Mr. Singh coaxed. "This is Captain Corbin. Master of the *Seven Seas*."

Sinbad stiffened.

"The *Seven Seas*," Mr. Singh repeated urgently.

Sinbad sounded odd when he said, "Call home the sailing ships."

Mr. Singh turned his head and glanced absently directly at the door behind which we were hiding. I was sure he had discovered us, but he was only staring blankly into space.

"Call home the sailing ships?" He was puzzled.

So were we.

"What kind of a clue is that?" I asked Nora. I don't mind telling you I was frustrated. My clue about the mandarin robe still seemed to me to make sense.

I jumped when Nora poked me.

"Cut that out!" I was annoyed. Couldn't she see I was thinking?

She poked me again, harder. "Harvey! Look at Butch. He's been hypnotized, too!"

I couldn't believe it. Butch was stiff as a board, his head partially raised, with a look in his eyes that showed he was in a complete fog. I had never even noticed, and I was sure neither had Mr. Singh. But trust Nora to be alert where an animal is concerned. Now she was furious.

"He ought to be in jail. Hypnotizing poor dumb animals. I think I'll go in there and tell him exactly what . . . let go of me, Harvey."

I had her in a tight grip, and wasn't about to let go.

At that moment, Mr. Singh counted to

three, and snapped his fingers. Butch came back to life, shook himself all over as if to rid himself of a feeling of strangeness, and yawned.

Sinbad squawked, ruffled his feathers, then gave his familiar maniacal laugh. "There's a sucker born every minute," he cackled, and laughed again.

Mr. Singh didn't know what to make of that, but I figured Captain Corbin had added that to confuse my uncle Buck.

It seemed to me that Mr. Singh was about to leave the room. I yanked Nora's arm and pulled her quickly back to the stairway and up a few steps, then turned her so it would appear we were just coming down. We had just come down one step when Mr. Singh appeared in the doorway.

"Ah. The young gentleman and the young miss," he greeted us. "I have a small favor to ask. Would it be possible for me to see Captain Corbin's room, just to see where he spent so many happy hours?"

"Sure," I said. Nora frowned at me, but I couldn't see how I could refuse without letting him know how suspicious we were.

As we started to go up the steps, Butch barked. He had come out of the living room and stretched out forlornly at the foot of the steps. I could see how longingly he gazed upwards. I felt so sorry for him. I figured he was probably remembering how easily he had raced up and down when he was a puppy. But Mr. Singh was walking up quickly, and I had to rush to keep pace.

As we climbed up, Mr. Singh questioned me. "You are, of course, most familiar with this house?" When I nodded, he went on, "I noticed, on my arrival, that a river runs beyond the house, does it not?"

I nodded again.

"And do you at times have a regatta, that is to say, a boat race festival, perhaps of sailing ships?"

"No, sir. I've never seen a sailing ship on this river."

He bit down on his lip, then said quickly, with a small smile, "An idle question, of no consequence."

When we began to walk down the long hallway, Nora nudged me in the back, then frowned heavily. She was dead set against our taking him to Captain Corbin's room, but I was determined to find out what he was really looking for there.

As we passed the last bedroom in the hall, I pointed it out. "That will be your room while you're here."

When I continued walking, then turned the sharp right angle, Mr. Singh was surprised. He commented, "How singular that a room should be rather hidden from sight."

Well, I wasn't about to tell him how important it had been in the past to have this room situated exactly the way it was. Or reveal anything about the secret door in the wardrobe, or the hidden stairway. And you better believe Nora wouldn't give him even the time of day, if she felt it would help him in any way.

When we entered the room, he stood stock still, only moving to study intently each and every item there. At last he swung around and saw the model sailing ship on the headboard of the bed. He drew his breath in so fast, it made a small, hissing sound. Then he bowed his head, almost prayerfully, and asked, "If I could have a moment alone here? So many memories, you understand."

"I don't think," Nora began.

He turned toward her swiftly, and for a moment there was a flash of anger in his eyes. I could feel a small shiver run through me, but it came and went so quickly, I thought I had imagined it. Maybe it was just the way the light slanted in from the window that caused him to appear so menacing.

Before he could say anything, I said, "Of course you can have time to yourself. I can understand that. We'll wait for you downstairs."

"You are most thoughtful." He bowed his head again, and didn't lift it to see if we left the room.

Outside I had to clamp my hand over Nora's mouth to keep her quiet. I just shoved her across the hall and behind a shuttered closet door, where we could peer out through the cracks.

"What's the matter with you?" I demanded. "You want him to know that we think he's up to something?"

Nora sputtered angrily. "You bet, Harvey. I want him to know. That way he won't try anything. And as soon as your Uncle Buck comes back, I think we should tell him . . ."

"What?" I interrupted. "That he hypnotized Sinbad? That's not a crime, Nora."

Nora couldn't believe I said that. "Not a crime to hypnotize a bird? And incidentally a dog at the same time? These are innocent *animals* we're talking about, Harvey. Besides, you don't know what he'll do in there."

"Like what?" I wanted to know. "Even if he searches the wardrobe, he won't find the secret door. And even if he did find the door by accident, what difference would it make? He'd sneak down and all he'd see is an empty room. Big deal."

Nora pinched me. "Shhhhh! He's coming out."

He opened the door stealthily, peered out, turned, and closed the door to Captain Corbin's room. Then he tiptoed to the corner, studied the hall furtively, and moved on at last, to disappear around the bend.

But not before we saw what he carried in his hands.

It was the model sailing ship.

Nora was so upset, she didn't know whether to shout at him, or cry.

"Call home the sailing ships." Tears began to spill from her eyes. "He got the clue. And now he has the treasure."

We just stood there, looking at one another helplessly.

It was a black moment.

8

In which the treasure is found . . . and lost

Nora gave me a vicious jab in the ribs with her fingers. "Well, what do we do now? Just stand here and let him get away with it?" she demanded.

I understood that she was so mad at Mr. Singh, she was taking her anger out on me. But a jab in the ribs hurts, and I didn't see why I had to be a stand-in for Mr. Singh.

I started to shove her back, just to show her there were plenty of hard feelings. After all, she's got strong fingers, and I have sensitive ribs. But I thought better of it, because the real hiding place of the treasure had suddenly exploded in my mind.

Cautioning her not to make a sound, I sneaked out of the closet, with Nora a close second behind me. I tiptoed past Mr. Singh's bedroom, down the hall to the steps.

"Where are we going?" Nora wanted to know.

"Downstairs," I explained. "To the kitchen. Where we can talk without *him*" — I jerked my head toward Mr. Singh's bedroom — "hearing us."

We made it to the kitchen all right, with Butch lumbering after us. His heart was in his eyes. Imagine! We'd been gone forever, as far as he was concerned. Dogs are like that. You can walk out the door, and walk right back in again, and a dog will go crazy with delight. Butch has always been like that. When he was younger, he'd leap all over me, drown me in slobbering kisses with his long tongue, glue himself to my side, and bark, as if to say, "Where've you *been*? What took you so long?"

When we had gone upstairs, he sank into deep dog misery. When we came down again, he was back in dog heaven. And now we were going into the kitchen — dog bliss! There was no way I wasn't going to give him a snack.

Nora and I decided to make some peanut butter sandwiches to eat during our pow-wow. I had jelly on mine, which is what you're supposed to put on peanut butter. Nora sliced a banana on hers.

"You'll be fat as a house," she told me, with a superior air. "Jelly is loaded with sugar. A banana is a natural source of . . ."

"You want to know where the treasure is, or don't you?" I interrupted.

I get enough lectures from my mom on eating sensibly. I don't need a cousin — a *skinny* girl cousin — to tell me what to do.

Part of Nora's sandwich fell on the floor. Butch gobbled it up, moaning with delight.

I paid no attention.

"Listen, Nora," I told her. "Mr. Singh won't find the treasure in that model ship."

Nora's eyes lit up as if I had just given her a present. "He won't? It isn't in the model ship? How do you know for sure, Harvey?"

"Because of the clue. Do you remember it?" I asked.

"Call home the sailing ships," she answered promptly.

"What's the key word?" I felt so triumphant I wished my arm was long enough so I could pat myself on the back.

Nora frowned. She was puzzled. "Call home," she repeated. "Home?"

When I shook my head back and forth and grinned at her, she exploded. "I hate when you do that, Harvey Willson. Don't try to show me how smart you are. Just..."

I had to interrupt her again. "Ships. Not *a* ship. *Ships*, plural," I explained loftily.

"Big deal," Nora muttered. "I don't see what you're so smug about. I don't see any ships around here. Plural," she added, glowering at me.

"Don't you remember?" I acted surprised. "Didn't I tell you that Captain Corbin used to make *ships* and put them in bottles?"

"Ohhhhh! Harvey, you're a genius!" She was awed by my brilliance.

I didn't rub it in. After all, I still needed her help.

"Then the model sailing ship was a false clue," she went on gleefully. "I bet he's real mad by now."

"The thing for us to do is sneak up to Uncle Buck's room," I began.

"Most clever," said a voice. It was no longer silky but sharp and dangerous as an ice pick.

We swung around. Mr. Singh leaned in the doorway, a small smile on his lips. Smiles are supposed to show warm feelings, but this one chilled me.

Nora blurted out, "It's not polite to listen in on other people's conversations. I thought Indians were polite."

"Oh yes, young miss. Most polite. And now I will request, politely, of course" — he bowed in her direction — "that you both accompany me upstairs to the room of the uncle Buck."

"You don't need us for that," Nora told him quickly. "All you have to do is go to the fourth bedroom on the right."

Mr. Singh's smile grew frostier.

"And leave you behind to call your uncle Buck? Or the police? You will come with me now."

I started to say, "Make me," but changed my mind when I saw what suddenly appeared in his hand.

"You have a gun!" Nora was stunned.

So was I.

It's one thing to see people waving guns around on television. But when a real gun is aimed directly at you, your stomach drops to your toes, and your mouth goes all dry.

We got up from the table, walked silently to the door, past Mr. Singh, and up the steps slowly. Butch took up his vigil at the foot of the stairway, and, like a good watchdog, went happily to sleep.

I couldn't help wishing there were six stories to the house, plus an attic, and that Uncle Buck's room was way, way up, but we made it to his room in seconds. I opened the door and waited, but Mr. Singh waved Nora and me to go ahead.

When he caught sight of the cabinet, with its shelves loaded with ships in bottles, he drew in a deep breath. I have to admit that it is an impressive sight. There were ships of all sizes — small, medium, large. Even Nora's eyes grew wide and solemn when she saw them.

"The cabinet is locked," I told Mr. Singh hopefully.

"Then we shall open it, shall we not?" he

replied agreeably. He smashed the glass near the lock with his gun, reached in, and opened the door.

Nora was shocked. "That's vandalism. Didn't anybody teach you manners over there in India?"

"Nora," I practically hissed at her.

You don't tell a man with a gun in his hand that his manners are terrible.

Mr. Singh only seemed amused.

"I will send your good uncle an apology. Meanwhile, remove the bottles and place them on the bed."

We did what he asked, unwillingly, but carefully.

"Now. Hold a bottle, one at a time, up to the light," Mr. Singh ordered.

Again we obeyed. When the last bottle was back on the bed, he was both angry and mystified.

No treasure was visible.

"This is dumb!" Nora exclaimed. "We don't even know what the treasure is."

Mr. Singh didn't seem to mind explaining. "But, my dear young miss, is it not obvious? We are looking for precious gems."

I never felt so helpless. I knew exactly where the gems were, but I didn't dare say so. I guess, though, that I couldn't keep a knowing gleam out of my eyes, for Nora caught my expression, turned to the bottles, then shouted triumphantly, "Of course, Harvey. The corks!"

If she had been close enough, I would have jabbed her so hard with my elbow it would have gone right through her body. She realized the moment the words were out of her mouth what she had done. Her face turned red, and she clapped her hand over her lips.

I shook my head. That was Nora all right. Whatever was on the tip of her mind was instantly on the tip of her tongue.

Well, the damage was done now.

Mr. Singh treated her to a dazzling smile of approval.

"Now then, young miss, and you, too, young master. Remove the corks most carefully."

So we did, and for once I wasn't happy to know that I was right.

The corks had been specially made by Captain Corbin to split in two when they were removed from the bottles. In seconds, a large diamond, a huge blood-red ruby, a black pearl, a luminous opal, a bright blue sapphire, and a brilliant green emerald lay in a radiant pool of color on the white bedspread.

Mr. Singh scooped them up and dropped them into his pocket.

We'd found the treasure, only to lose it now, forever.

9

In which a bird swallows an eye

Nora, being Nora, blurted out angrily, "Well, I hope you're satisfied."

"More than satisfied," Mr. Singh began, but Nora interrupted him.

"I bet you're the kind who steals towels from hotel rooms. I bet you steal candy from babies. I bet . . ."

"Where are *your* manners, young miss?" Mr. Singh scolded. "Is this the way you are taught, to insult a guest in your home?"

He pointed the gun at her.

"Don't shoot!" I yelled.

Nora stared at him, shocked into silence.

"Bid her to be quiet then," Mr. Singh snapped at me. "I have little patience with young girls who babble."

"She's upset," I explained, "because you're stealing Uncle Buck's treasure."

"But he is an old man. What need has he of treasure?" Mr. Singh studied us for a moment. "Now, what to do with you?" he muttered to himself.

"We could just stay right here," I offered hopefully.

Mr. Singh clicked his tongue against his teeth, making small *tsk, tsk, tsk* sounds. "No." He came to a decision. "In a house of this size, there is most certainly a basement . . ."

"Not in the basement," Nora wailed. "I hate basements."

He ignored her. "There I shall tie you up," he continued, "and there perhaps your uncle will find you and free you eventually. If he thinks to look in the basement," he added thoughtfully.

Having made this decision, Mr. Singh used his gun to motion us toward the door.

"You're not a very nice person," Nora told him angrily as we left the room and marched down the hall to the steps.

Mr. Singh laughed. "Now that I have

found what I came for, and will take with me when I leave, I will change my ways. It is easy to be nice when one is rich." He patted his pocket.

As we began to go down the steps, with Mr. Singh a step above us, Nora frowned at me. "Do something, Harvey." She mouthed the words at me, exaggerating her lip movements so I would have no trouble reading them.

"Like what?" I mouthed back at her.

She gave me an impatient glare and took things into her own hands. She stopped so suddenly halfway down that Mr. Singh almost ran into her.

"I think I'm going to be sick," she announced triumphantly. "I think I'm going to throw up." She made a loud gagging noise.

I don't know about you, but I can never hear someone do that without wanting to throw up, too. I clapped my hand over my mouth and inhaled a deep breath through my nose.

Mr. Singh wasn't bothered the least bit. He just pressed the gun into her back and said, "I encourage you to change your mind."

He prodded her with the gun, and then prodded me, so we continued down the steps as slowly as we could. My mind was racing. I didn't want to be tied up, especially in a dark and musty basement.

We had to stop him. We couldn't let him get away with the treasure. We just couldn't. But what could either of us do? Then I saw Butch at the foot of the steps, standing there with his tongue hanging out as he panted with joy to see us again.

All of a sudden, I had a wild idea.

On the second step from the bottom, I shoved Nora hard. She went tumbling down and hit the floor. At the same time, I yelled, "SIC 'EM, BUTCH. GO GET HIM."

Butch hadn't heard those words from me for a long time, but I counted on his remembering them somehow.

Mr. Singh promptly struck me with the back of his hand. "Do not provoke me further," he warned. "Move on."

Butch had made it up the first step. When Mr. Singh hit me, Butch growled deep in his throat. He leaped forward and buried his teeth into Mr. Singh's left leg. He missed the

bone, but he got a firm grip on the cloth.
Butch yanked so hard, Mr. Singh lost his balance. He tripped, flailed his arms in the air,
and sailed over Butch to land with a hard
thump on the floor.

At that moment, we heard Uncle Buck's
voice.

"Harvey. Nora," he called. "Myrtle stayed
on to help your mom. I came back to see
if . . ."

He walked into the hall, with Sinbad on
his shoulder, and stopped short when he saw
Mr. Singh out cold at the foot of the steps.

"*Freeze!*" Sinbad screamed. "*Nobody
move. I've got you covered.*"

Uncle Buck was stunned. "What's going
on here?" he wanted to know. "What happened to Mr. Singh?"

Before either Nora or I could explain,
Butch got back into the act. He hadn't had
this much excitement in his life since he got
his head stuck in the fence and was rescued
by the fire department. Now he moved closer
to Mr. Singh, snarling as if he'd turned wolf,
and buried his teeth into Mr. Singh's turban.
He gave it a hard tug, and looked surprised

when the turban practically flew off. Butch flopped down on the floor and worried at the turban, biting and shaking it and making low growling sounds in his throat.

I couldn't believe what I saw. Under that turban Mr. Singh hadn't hidden long dark hair. Instead, Mr. Singh's hair was quite short, and curly, and so blond it was almost white.

Nora folded her arms and glared at him. "He's not an Indian. He never was!"

Mr. Singh moaned and opened his eyes. And we all received another shock. He had one brilliant blue eye, which didn't match his other deep brown eye. He made an attempt to get up, then put his hand to his forehead.

"My head," he groaned. His hand moved up to adjust his turban, and he said in a startled voice, "I've lost my turban!"

"There's something else you've lost, mister," Uncle Buck informed him coldly. "Your eyes don't match anymore. You've lost a contact lens, haven't you?"

"I can explain," Mr. Singh said quickly. He began to grope along the floor, his long fingers covering the area all around him.

"Will somebody help me, please?" he pleaded.

I guess Sinbad took that as an invitation. He flew down, picked up the gleaming brown lens, which he had spotted with his sharp eyes, flew back to Uncle Buck's shoulder, and then calmly gulped down the lens.

"My eye!" Mr. Singh exclaimed. "He swallowed my eye!"

He started to get up again. From the expression on his face, I had a feeling he was itching to get his hands around Sinbad's neck.

"Nora!" I yelled. "You're closest. Grab the gun! It's right behind your feet."

For an old man, Uncle Buck can move fast when he wants to, for he was next to Nora in a second, scooping up the gun before she could. He stared down at the weapon in his hand, then exploded.

"You brought a gun into my house? How dare you!"

I thought for a minute Uncle Buck was about to grab Mr. Singh and shake him until his teeth rattled.

Sinbad, who had been startled by Uncle

Buck's sudden move, had flown up to the chandelier. Now he perched on it upside down, and asked, sounding exactly like Uncle Buck, "In my house? How dare you!"

Nora explained, glancing from Uncle Buck up to Sinbad, as if she thought they both should know, "It was awful! He was going to shoot us, because he's got the treasure. It's in his pocket."

Uncle Buck repeated, "The treasure?" as if they were words in a foreign language. I could understand his bewilderment. He had never believed there was a treasure to begin with. Then what Nora had said seemed to penetrate his mind, because he became furious. "*Shoot* you? He threatened to *shoot* you?"

Uncle Buck aimed the gun at Mr. Singh. "We'll see who shoots who around here."

Sinbad flew down and landed on Uncle Buck's arm. That made Uncle Buck's finger tighten on the trigger. There was a loud popping sound, then a jet stream of water hit Mr. Singh in his mouth just as he opened it to explain.

"A water gun! You pulled a water gun on us," Nora exploded.

Mr. Singh looked at her as if it should have been obvious right away. "Naturally," he told her. "Real guns are dangerous."

"Who are you anyway, mister?" Uncle Buck wanted an explanation, and he wanted it *now*.

Mr. Singh tried to get up again.

"Butch!" I ordered. "SIT!" I pointed at Mr. Singh. Butch may be old and lazy, but he still knows the bad guys from the good guys. He walked right up to Mr. Singh, plopped down on top of him real hard, turned his head so his eyes looked right into Mr. Singh's, and showed his teeth.

Mr. Singh made a small sound, *whumpf*, like a collapsing balloon. Well, after all, Butch is really big, and heavy.

"We ought to tie him up," I said, turning to Uncle Buck.

He didn't answer. He seemed frozen, as if suddenly made of stone. His head was turned upward; there was a blank look in his eyes.

"What's the matter?" I asked urgently.

"Harvey! Look!" Nora whispered, and pointed.

So I glanced upward, too.

A figure stood motionless at the top of the stairway. I couldn't see it clearly, for it was enveloped in shadow. One thing I could make out, however. The figure wore the mandarin robe. In its right hand was clutched the scimitar from the wall in Captain Corbin's room.

"Jack?" Uncle Buck said in a hushed voice. "Is that you, Jack Corbin?"

He clutched his chest and swayed. His face grew pale, and I thought he would faint dead away.

10

In which a finder is not a keeper

As the figure slowly came down the steps, I knew it couldn't be anyone else but Captain Corbin. He was just as Uncle Buck had described him to me.

He had the look of a man of the sea. His lids narrowed over his keen gray eyes, as if to shield them from a blazing sun. His face was weatherbeaten, the skin leathery and tanned, with a fan of wrinkles at each eye. He was tall, taller than my dad, with strong shoulders, a stocky body, and powerful hands. I could easily imagine Captain Corbin battling stormy seas and howling winds.

"You're supposed to be dead," Nora announced. She was delighted. Her eyes glowed; her expression was expectant.

Later, Nora told me she visualized him as a samurai warrior, dressed as he was in the mandarin robe with a broad, colorful sash across his middle, and the scimitar sharp and wicked in his right hand.

Of course I was tickled to be able to point out loftily that samurai warriors are Japanese who wouldn't be caught dead in a *Chinese* mandarin robe.

"I knew that all the time, Harvey," she lied. "I was just testing to see if you did."

Would you believe she told me that without so much as blinking an eye?

Butch was so interested he forgot about guarding Mr. Singh. He came close to me, and wagged his tail as he looked upward. Mr. Singh took advantage of that to leap to his feet. He cast a worried glance at Captain Corbin and tried to run from the room.

Captain Corbin bounded down the steps and was at Mr. Singh's side in a flash.

"Not so fast, Paddy," Captain Corbin said, and laid the scimitar gently but firmly across Mr. Singh's chest. His voice was mild, but his gray eyes were grim. He forced Mr. Singh back to a chair against the wall. Butch

must have gotten a new surge of energy because he stationed himself at the chair and
bared his teeth. I think Butch enjoyed being
a real dog again, even for a little while.

Sinbad flew to Captain Corbin, sat on his
shoulder, and repeated Uncle Buck's words.
"Jack? Is that you, Jack Corbin?"

Uncle Buck smiled. It was good to see his
face its normal color again. His eyes were
bright and cheerful.

"I knew you weren't dead, Jack. I never
believed it for one minute," Uncle Buck told
him. Then he glared at Mr. Singh. "This fellow told me you died in his arms. Even gave
me your ring, Jack, to prove it."

"He stole it from me, Buck, when I was
unconscious in the hospital in the bed next to
him." There was contempt in his voice.

Mr. Singh sounded apologetic when he explained, "Well, Jacko, I did need the ring,
you see. How else could I have convinced
the old man to let me in so I could search for
the treasure?"

"Who is this guy, anyway?" Uncle Buck
asked. "He's no Indian."

Mr. Singh introduced himself with a smile.

It was odd to see one twinkling blue eye and one shiny brown eye. "My name is Patrick O'Gowan. But my friends call me Paddy. Isn't that right, Jacko me boy?"

It was strange to think of Patrick O'Gowan instead of Mr. Singh. He sure had convinced us, not only with his looks but the way he mimicked the singsong Indian way of speaking.

"You came to rob me, and Jack, and have the nerve to use the word *friend*?" Uncle Buck was angry. "Well, *friend*, I'll take the treasure now."

"Surely not." Paddy O'Gowan sounded surprised. "Be reasonable, my dear fellow. I solved the clue . . ."

"You did not!" Nora shouted. "Harvey did. You listened and then you forced us to . . ."

Paddy O'Gowan shrugged. "The child is hysterical. No matter. You know what they say, Jacko. Finders keepers. You'll not deny that surely."

I stared at Paddy O'Gowan and my jaw dropped. He was like a slippery eel. The Indian singsong was not only gone, it was replaced with the lilting speech of an Irishman.

"He pulled a gun on us," I told Captain Corbin.

Again Paddy O'Gowan leaped in to explain.

"A water gun." He laughed. "Can you see taking me to court, then? And telling his honor I threatened them with a *water* gun? I'd never have harmed them."

"You were going to tie us up and leave us in the basement," Nora accused him.

Paddy O'Gowan shook his head. "Never. On my solemn oath." He shrank back in his seat when Uncle Buck took a step closer with rage in his eyes.

"Call the police, Jack," he commanded.

Paddy O'Gowan said quickly, "I did save your life, Jacko. Why don't you tell him that, laddie?"

Captain Corbin nodded. "I'll give you that, Paddy. You saved my life . . ."

"At great risk to my own," Paddy O'Gowan interrupted.

"At great risk to your own," Captain Corbin agreed. He turned to the rest of us and said, "It was during the shipwreck. I suffered a concussion, lost consciousness, and went under. Paddy here held me afloat though he was badly injured himself. He dragged me ashore on some nameless island and tended me until we were rescued." Captain Corbin rapped his knuckles on his head. "They had to replace part of my skull with this steel plate."

Nora and I were fascinated. We'd never ever met anybody who had a steel plate in his head.

"We were a long time in the hospital. When I finally was able to speak, we spent long hours, Paddy and I, talking. And that was when I told him about the treasure. Not where it was hidden, only that Sinbad had the clue. He was my friend, Buck. He had been my friend for a long time at sea."

"And yet you didn't trust me, Jacko," Paddy put in reproachfully. "Never once did you tell me what the clue was. That hurt, Jacko."

"*Trust* you?" Uncle Buck was astonished. "Trust *you*?"

"Well, we were friends. Friends don't

keep secrets from one another." Paddy O'Gowan sounded upset.

"My good and true friend put something in my food that knocked me out. And while I slept," Captain Corbin shook his head as if he still couldn't believe it, "he slipped the ring off my finger. When I awoke, he was gone. I knew where he was headed, for sure."

Captain Corbin turned to stare with a cold eye at Paddy O'Gowan. "Did you think I wouldn't know you in that Indian disguise? And the dyed beard and mustache?"

"I thought I was very convincing. Everybody here thought I was a real Sikh. I fooled you, didn't I, old man?"

Uncle Buck's face reddened. He hates being called old.

I only half-listened, because something else was on my mind. I blurted out, "Captain, you were in the boathouse, weren't you?"

Captain Corbin nodded.

"I came through the tunnel from the boathouse, up the stairway, into my room. It was good to be back there, Buck. Home at last,

I told myself. And I put on this robe." He smoothed the fabric gratefully with his left hand. "I'd forgotten how warm and comfortable it is. I had just lit my pipe when I heard voices."

"That was us," Nora said.

Captain Corbin smiled at her. "So I had to beat a hasty retreat. Back through the secret door in the wardrobe, down the steps to the hidden room. I thought I would linger there until you two were gone, so I lit the hurricane lamp. I never expected you to come down there, you see. Then there you were, whispering on the steps. So I blew out the candle and got back to the boathouse as fast as I could."

"Did you oil the door so it wouldn't squeak?" I wanted to know.

"I brought an oilcan from the boathouse," Captain Corbin explained. "I couldn't take a chance on having that door squeak."

Nora sighed.

I did, too.

Three mysteries were cleared up — the silent door, the mandarin robe, and the warm hurricane lamp.

Paddy O'Gowan stirred restlessly. "I'm sure this is all very interesting, Jacko. What is more to the point at the moment is, what do you plan to do now? Where do I stand, eh, old friend?"

Captain Corbin stared at Paddy O'Gowan for a long moment. Then he said in a brooding voice, "What, indeed? What do I do with you now?"

11

In which there is a safe harbor

"I've done no one harm," Patrick O'Gowan said with a smile. "And after all, Jacko, if you stop to think of it, old friend, it was you that put temptation in my path."

"Me?" Captain Corbin was surprised.

"Babbling on about the treasure," O'Gowan told him reproachfully. "And me with a weakness, you might say, for the good life."

Paddy O'Gowan looked at Uncle Buck as if asking for approval. "What was a man to do then?" he asked.

"Ignore him," Uncle Buck said, turning to Captain Corbin. "You were saying you went back to the boathouse . . ."

"And went back to my room when I thought the little ones would be gone."

"Little one?" Nora repeated, insulted. "I'm an inch and a half taller than Harvey. And I'm halfway through fifth grade."

I was insulted, too.

"Who figured out the answer to the riddle of the treasure?" I demanded. "*This* little kid, that's who."

"I beg your pardon," Captain Corbin said. "To continue, Buck. When I returned to my room, I heard voices down here. By the time I reached the head of the stairway, I saw Paddy here tripping head over heels onto the floor, and that very large dog sitting astride him."

Paddy O'Gowan was restless. "There's no need for me to linger now, is there, old friend? I've a mind to be going now."

"Going?" Uncle Buck roared. "The only place you're going is to jail."

Captain Corbin shook his head. "No, Buck. He saved my life. I owe him for that."

Paddy O'Gowan's face was one broad smile. He leaped up from the chair. I guess

Butch hadn't been listening to the conversation. As far as Butch knew, Paddy O'Gowan was still one of the bad guys. So Butch sank his teeth, lightly but firmly, into Paddy O'Gowan's leg.

"Will you call off the brute?" Paddy O'Gowan requested. "And you'll see me no more, I promise."

"Not so fast, friend." Captain Corbin frowned. "First I'll relieve you of the jewels."

"You're a hard man, Jack Corbin." Paddy O'Gowan slipped his hand reluctantly into his pocket. He sighed. "To be so close, and to be booby-trapped by children. Unfair, that's what it is."

Paddy O'Gowan put the gems into Captain Corbin's outstretched hand. With a last woeful glance, and a sigh for the treasure that had almost been his, Paddy O'Gowan waited for Butch to release him. I pulled Butch away, and I told him he was the best dog in the whole world and ought to have a medal. Butch gave me a few long loving licks with his tongue, and settled down near the steps again.

Meanwhile, Paddy O'Gowan scooped up

his turban, placed it firmly on his head, walked to the front door, opened it, gave us all a brilliant smile, and was gone.

We followed Captain Corbin into the dining room, where he spread out the jewels on the table. With the overhead chandelier all lit up, the gems seemed to catch fire, glowing and sparkling in a way that made us catch our breath.

Finally, Uncle Buck said, "You can make a whole new life for yourself, Jack. You can retire a rich man."

Captain Corbin laughed. "Retire? Maybe so. But not like you mean. This house. I know what pride you take in it. We'll try to have it declared a national treasure. We'll restore it as much as possible to the way it was when it was part of the Underground Railroad. And we'll offer to maintain it as well."

Uncle Buck's eyes filled with tears. Well, I told you, didn't I? He's a man who cries easily.

"My great-grandfather helped slaves to a new life from this old house. I'd like that to be remembered. Did you know that one of the slaves, a man named Aaron, wrote to my great-grandfather after he reached Halifax in Nova Scotia?"

Nora and I looked at each other.

Free at last Aaron 1859. That was what he had carved into the table in the hidden room.

Uncle Buck went on, "He said he and the others would never forget that there had been people who cared. He wrote that he had taken a new name, and wanted my great-grandfather to remember it. *Free man*. Aaron Freeman."

Nora's eyes grew misty. For once she had nothing to say.

I felt kind of misty-eyed myself. I remembered the shadows on the wall. Maybe now those shadows would always be there.

"And that isn't all," Captain Corbin continued. "You know that big meadow out back?"

Uncle Buck nodded.

"Buck, you and I are going to build a home on that land. For men who can no longer go to sea. We're going to give them a safe harbor."

I liked those words. This house had been

a safe harbor. Now there would be another kind of safe harbor on Uncle Buck's land. Uncle Buck and Captain Corbin would see to that.

I turned aside to whisper to Nora. "Aren't you glad you had to spend your holidays with us?"

"I sure am," she told me. "And the best part of all was Sinbad."

"Better than the treasure? You're kidding."

She gave me a pitying look, as if she didn't expect me to be able to understand.

"Sinbad is the real treasure, Harvey."

Well, maybe that was one way of looking at it. Maybe it was the only way for Nora. I think, when Nora is grown up, she'll go live in a jungle and study gorillas, or chimpanzees. Or maybe work in a zoo where she can care for all kinds of animals.

"My mom and dad will sure be surprised when we tell them about our adventure," I said. I was even looking forward to dinner tonight, so I could fill them in on all the excitement they missed. And Myrtle Crump's bracelets and bells and bangles would jingle and jangle all over the place when she heard that her handsome Sikh was a fake.

I could hardly wait for suppertime to come.

Nora was busy with her own thoughts. Now she told me, "When I go home and tell everybody about everything that's happened, they won't believe a word I say."

I nodded.

"Funny, isn't it?" I asked. "How you always get me mixed up in some kind of weird happening every time you visit?"

Her jaw dropped. "ME? I get *you* mixed up, Harvey Willson? If that isn't just like a boy."

But it's true just the same, even if she doesn't think so.

I just gave her one of my best superior looks, and then I said to Uncle Buck, "I'm starved. When do we eat lunch?"

Butch beat us to the kitchen with minutes to spare.